Spotter's Guide to
DOGS

Harry Glover

Illustrated by John Francis

Contents

The editors would like to thank
Peter Messent and Peter Kendall
of KalKan Animals Studies Center,
and Dr Jane Sparracino, for their
help and advice.

Editorial Director
Sue Jacquemier

Editors
Rosamund Kidman Cox,
Tim Dowley

First published in 1979 by Usborne Publishing
Limited, Usborne House, 83-85 Saffron Hill,
London EC1N 8RT

How to use this book

This book is an identification guide to dog breeds. Take it with you when you go out spotting or when you visit a dog show.

Originally most dog breeds were bred to do a certain job, so in this book the breeds are arranged in groups according to the jobs they were used for, such as herding, guarding or hunting.

Next to each picture of a dog is a short description of the breed. It tells you which country the breed comes from and the dog's coloring. The normal height of the breed is given in inches.

Beside each dog is a small blank circle. When you spot a breed make a check in the correct circle. The scorecard at the end of the book gives a score for each breed. Common breeds score 5 points and rare ones 25.

At the back of the book you will find information about buying and looking after a dog.

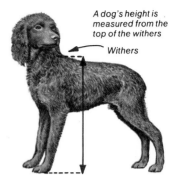

A dog's height is measured from the top of the withers

Withers

Dog breeds

The dogs in this book come from all over the world, but most of their ancestors came from Europe and the Far East. They were originally bred for special purposes such as hunting game or pulling sleds, and this is how the pedigree breeds began. The map below shows you the main dog breeding areas of the world today.

The main dog breeding areas of the world

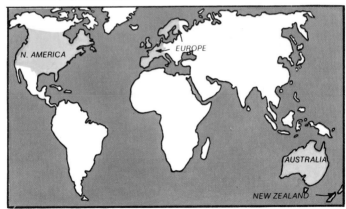

N. AMERICA   EUROPE

AUSTRALIA

NEW ZEALAND

Looking at dogs

In this book you will find information about many dog breeds. Some of the special words that are used to describe them are illustrated on these pages; others are explained in the glossary on page 59.

The dog and the bitch
The male, or "dog", is usually stronger and often larger than the female, or "bitch". Sometimes he is more aggressive and may wander.

A bitch is more likely to become attached to one person. She will probably stay closer to home.

A bitch is ready to mate two or three times a year; these are called her "heat periods." When she is "in heat" she becomes restless, bleeds a little from her vulva and may want to wander to find a mate. She stays like this for about three weeks. She then returns to her normal way of life unless she has mated.

Naming the parts of a dog
The parts of a dog are given special names; you may hear them in use if you go to a dog show. Some more words you might hear are:
Feathering – long fringes of hair on the body.

Racy – slightly built.
Cobby – heavy, with a short back.
Stern – the tail of some breeds.
Wall eyes – eyes of a different color, e.g., one blue, one white.

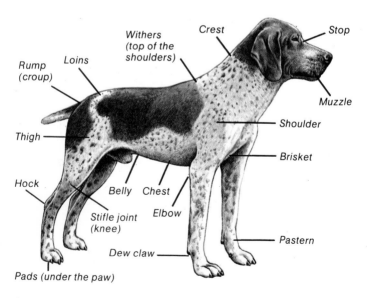

Crest

Stop

Withers (top of the shoulders)

Loins

Rump (croup)

Muzzle

Thigh

Shoulder

Brisket

Hock

Belly Chest

Elbow

Stifle joint (knee)

Dew claw

Pastern

Pads (under the paw)

Ears & tails

When you are learning to identify different breeds, look at the ears and tails. Some breeds hold their ears or tails in a distinctive way.

You may see some breeds with very short, docked tails. Docking – the shortening or removal of the tail – is carried out when the puppy is very young and is a virtually painless operation. The argument in favor of doing this is that long tails left on working dogs may become injured when the animal is working. However, some dogs have their tails docked for fashion reasons. Cropping – the removal of the flap of the ear – is not illegal in the USA.

Tail set high

Tail set low

Tail carried upright

Pendant (hanging) ears

Erect ears

Semi-erect ears

Curled tail

Long, flowing tail

Feathering

Running dogs

All the running dogs were once used to chase game. They have long legs and can run fast.

Saluki ▶
Originally from the Middle East where it was used to hunt deer and antelope. Has a smooth or feathered coat and long ears. Usually kept as a pet. White, golden, black and tan.
23-28 inches high.

Feathered, curved tail

Feathered tail

Feathered legs

◀ Borzoi
Originally from Russia, where the Czars used it to hunt game and wolves. Has a long, silky coat and a long tail.
Various colors.
28-30 inches high.

Afghan Hound ▶
Ancient breed. Once used to hunt small deer in Afghanistan. Long, silky coat and feathered ears. All colors.
27-29 inches high.

Long tail, curved at tip

Running dogs

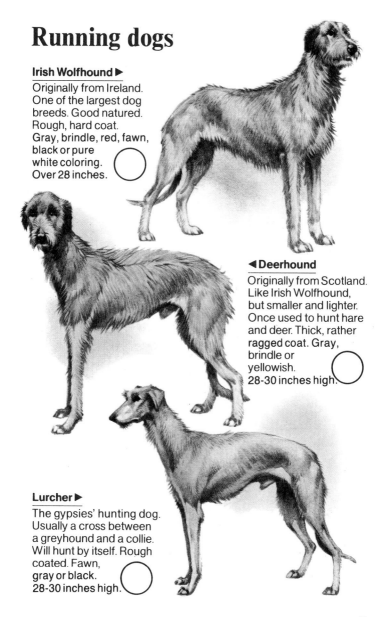

Irish Wolfhound ▶
Originally from Ireland.
One of the largest dog
breeds. Good natured.
Rough, hard coat.
Gray, brindle, red, fawn,
black or pure
white coloring.
Over 28 inches.

◀ Deerhound
Originally from Scotland.
Like Irish Wolfhound,
but smaller and lighter.
Once used to hunt hare
and deer. Thick, rather
ragged coat. Gray,
brindle or
yellowish.
28-30 inches high.

Lurcher ▶
The gypsies' hunting dog.
Usually a cross between
a greyhound and a collie.
Will hunt by itself. Rough
coated. Fawn,
gray or black.
28-30 inches high.

Running dogs

Pharaoh Hound ▶

Perhaps one of the oldest
breeds. Hunting dog from
the Mediterranean.
Smooth coat. Often rich
red, with white
on the chest.
21-25 inches high.

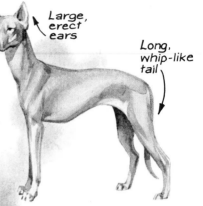

Large,
erect
ears

Long,
whip-like
tail

◀ Ibizan Hound

Originally from the island of
Ibiza. Used as a hunter and
watch dog. Rough or
smooth coat.
Various
colors.
24-26 inches high.

Sloughi ▶

Originally from North
Africa. A rare breed.
Easy to confuse with
the Saluki. Was used to
hunt small game. Has a
smooth coat. Usually
sandy, can be
brindle.
22-30 inches high.

Running dogs

Whippet ▶

Originally from North of England where bred for racing. Looks like a miniature Greyhound. Friendly. Smooth coated. Any color or color mixture. 17-19 inches high.

Curved back

Semi-erect ears folded back ←

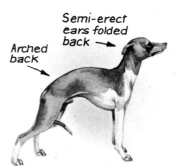

◀ Greyhound

Used for coursing by the Greeks and Romans. Can reach 50 mph. on the straight and used for track racing. Smooth coat. Most colors and color mixtures. 28-30 inches high.

Deep chest

Long, low-set tail

Italian Greyhound ▶

Originally from Italy. A toy dog and the smallest running dog. Smooth coat. Fawn, black, cream, white, pied. 12-14 inches high.

Semi-erect ears folded back →

Arched back →

Herding dogs

These dogs were originally bred to herd sheep and cattle; they may also have been guard dogs. Today only some of the breeds are used for herding.

Belgian Sheepdog ▶

Sheep dog from Belgium. Intelligent and obedient. Very good watch dog. Fairly long coat. Black coloring. 23-25 inches high.

Triangular and erect ears

Long neck hair

Triangular and erect ears

◀ Belgian Malinois

Belgian Shepherd Dog. Smooth coat, similar to German Shepherd Dog. Fawn or red coloring, with black hair-tips. 23-25 inches high.

Belgian Tervuren ▶

Comes from Belgium. Looks like Belgium Sheepdog, but is reddish-fawn with black hairtips and tailtip. 23-25 inches high.

Herding dogs

German Shepherd Dog/
Alsatian ▶

Bred from old European
shepherd dogs. Used by
police, armed forces and
as a guide dog for the blind.
Intelligent and easy to train.
Smooth coat. Can
be any color.
22-26 inches high.

*Triangular,
erect ears* ↘

*Tail hangs in a
slight curve* ↙

*Semi-erect
ears* ↘

◀ **Rough Collie**

Originally from Scotland
where it was used to herd
sheep; now also a show
dog. Long outer coat, short
undercoat. Usually sable
and white, tricolor, or blue
and white.
20-24 inches
high.

*Full
neck
ruff* ↑

*Semi-erect
ears* ←

Smooth Collie ▶

British breed. Less common
than Rough Collie; has a
short, hard,
smooth coat.
20-24 inches high.

Herding dogs

Old English Sheepdog ▶

British breed. Often called Bobtail. Good guard dog. Strong and active. Shaggy coat. Can be gray, blue or grizzle, with or without white markings. Over 22 inches high.

No tail ↙

Ears lie flat on the head ↘

← Beard on both sides of muzzle

◀ Bearded Collie

Originally from Scotland. Mainly used as a sheep dog. Long coat. Can be blue, gray to black, or red and white. 20-22 inches high.

← Semi-erect ears

Full neck ruff

Shetland Sheepdog ▶

Originally from the Shetland Islands. Looks like a small Collie. Has a long, hairy tail. Long coat. Colors include black and white, black and tan, merle, sable. 14-15 inches high.

Herding dogs

Komondor ▶
Originally from Hungary. Thick coat hangs in long cords. Bold, tough dog which can work in cold conditions.
Always white.
22-32 inches high.

Corded coat

Hair falls over the eyes

Curved tail →

Corded coat

Tail curled over the back

◀ Puli
Sheep dog from Hungary. Soft, woolly undercoat and long outer coat hanging in cords. Can work in cold conditions. White, gray or black.
15-17 inches high.

Tail curled over the back

Tibetan Terrier ▶
Originally from mountains of Tibet. Once used to herd sheep, goats and cattle. Lively, sporting dog. Long, fine, double coat. Can be white, cream, gray, golden and black.
14-16 inches high.

Large, round feet

Herding dogs

Briard ▶

French breed. Intelligent.
Square look to body. Long,
wavy, stiff coat. Can be
any color
except white.
22-27 inches high.

*Eyebrows hang
over the eyes* →

*Feathered, curved
tail* →

*Docked
tail*

*Short,
erect
ears*

◀ Bouvier des Flandres

Once used by Flemish
farmers to drive cattle.
Quick, active and easy to
train. Head hair forms
eyebrows, moustache and
beard. Rough, wiry coat.
Drab yellow, gray
or black coloring.
25-26 inches high.

*White
tip to
tail*

Border Collie ▶

Good working sheep dog;
very intelligent. Often seen
at sheep dog trials. Longish,
smooth or slightly wavy coat.
Usually black
and white.
20-21 inches high.

14

Herding dogs

Maremma ▶
Comes from Central Italy.
Used to herd and guard.
Friendly and intelligent.
Longish coat. Black nose.
Usually white; can have
lemon or
fawn markings.
24-27 inches high.

Long neck hair

◀ Kuvasz
Hunting dog from Hungary.
Used to herd sheep and
cattle.
Long neck hair; shorter,
wavy body hair.
Always white.
26-30 inches high.

Great Pyrenees ▶
Originally from the
Pyrenees in Southern
France. Once used to
guard animals against
wolves and bears. Large,
strong breed, with thick
coat. All white, or white
with
markings.
26-32 inches high.

Thick coat

Heeling dogs

These dogs have a special skill, they can all drive cattle. If the cattle stop, the dogs nip their heels, then back away before the animal can kick. This is why they are called "heelers."

Very short tail

Vallhund ▶
Comes from Sweden. Also called "Västgötaspets." Nearly died out in 1940s. Has a short coat. Can be gray, brownish or red in color.
15-19 inches high.

Very short tail

Erect ears →

◀ Pembroke Corgi
Originally used to drive cattle and ponies in South Wales; now a popular pet. Shortish coat. Can be red, black, fawn, or black and tan, or have some white markings.
10-12 inches high.

Large, erect ears point out →

Fox-like tail

Cardigan Corgi ▶
Another cattle driving dog from South Wales. Longer body and larger ears than Pembroke. Still used by Welsh farmers. Short coat. Any color except white.
12 inches high.

Heeling dogs

Kelpie ▶

Comes from Australia.
Bred from sheep dogs
and the Australian dingo
(a wild dog). Tough and
hard working. Short coat.
Black, red or
chocolate.
17-20 inches high.

Erect ears

Tail
curled
over
back
and to
one
side

◀ Norwegian Buhund

Farm dog from Norway.
Brave and intelligent.
Has a long, thick coat,
longest on body and neck.
Can be fawn, red
or yellowish.
18 inches high.

Speckled coat

Australian Cattle Dog ▶

Bred in Australia, from the
Smooth Collie, dingo
(wild dog) and Dalmatian.
Very strong. Used to drive
cattle. Short coat. Red
or blue
speckled.
18-20 inches high.

Guard dogs

These breeds are all good guard dogs, used for guarding people and places. They come from many parts of the world and some of them were originally hunting dogs.

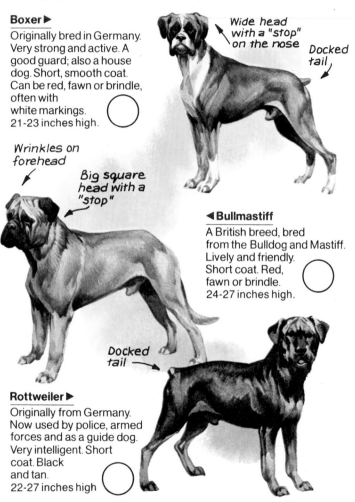

Boxer ▶

Originally bred in Germany. Very strong and active. A good guard; also a house dog. Short, smooth coat. Can be red, fawn or brindle, often with white markings. 21-23 inches high.

Wide head with a "stop" on the nose

Docked tail

Wrinkles on forehead

Big square head with a "stop"

◀ Bullmastiff

A British breed, bred from the Bulldog and Mastiff. Lively and friendly. Short coat. Red, fawn or brindle. 24-27 inches high.

Docked tail

Rottweiler ▶

Originally from Germany. Now used by police, armed forces and as a guide dog. Very intelligent. Short coat. Black and tan. 22-27 inches high

Guard dogs

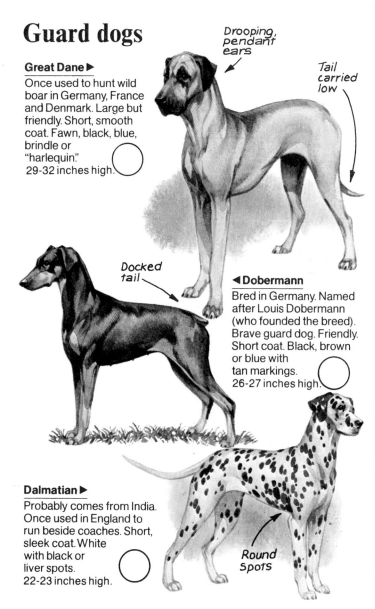

Drooping, pendant ears

Tail carried low

Great Dane ▶
Once used to hunt wild boar in Germany, France and Denmark. Large but friendly. Short, smooth coat. Fawn, black, blue, brindle or "harlequin." 29-32 inches high.

Docked tail

◀ Dobermann
Bred in Germany. Named after Louis Dobermann (who founded the breed). Brave guard dog. Friendly. Short coat. Black, brown or blue with tan markings. 26-27 inches high.

Dalmatian ▶
Probably comes from India. Once used in England to run beside coaches. Short, sleek coat. White with black or liver spots. 22-23 inches high.

Round spots

Guard dogs

Anatolian Karabash ▶

Originally from Turkey,
where it was used to guard
sheep. Short coat. Can
be cream, fawn,
brindle or black.
26-30 inches high.

◀ Leonberger

A rare German breed.
Friendly house dog and
a brave guard. Long
soft coat.
Golden to red.
27-31 inches high.

Estrela Mountain Dog ▶

Originally from the Estrela
Mountains in Portugal.
A rare breed. Strong,
intelligent and active.
Usually fawn,
black mask.
25-28 inches high.

Guard dogs

Newfoundland ▶

Originally from Newfound-
land. Good swimmer.
Very strong. Long coat.
Black, black and
white or bronze.
26-28 inches high.

Drooping
pendant
ears

Long,
weather-
resistant
coat

Large head
with square
muzzle

◀ Saint Bernard

Originally from the
St. Bernard Hospice in the
Swiss Alps where it has
been used to rescue
travelers lost in the snow.
Heavy and strong. Rough
or smooth coat.
Usually red
and white.
26-28 inches high.

Drooping
pendant
ears

Bernese Mountain Dog ▶

Originally from Switzerland
where it was used to pull
carts. Easy to train. Good
guard. Long, soft coat.
Black, brown or tan
markings,
white chest.
24-26 inches high.

Guard dogs

Giant Schnauzer ▶

Originally from Bavaria, Germany where it was used to herd cattle. Good guard dog. Wiry coat. Black or "salt-and-pepper" color. 28 inches high.

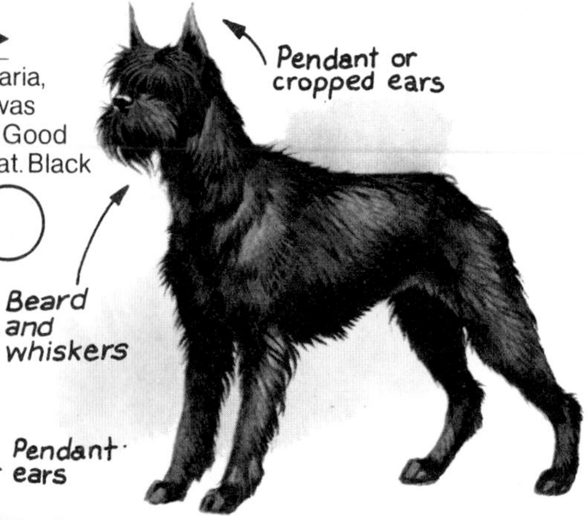

Pendant or cropped ears

Beard and whiskers

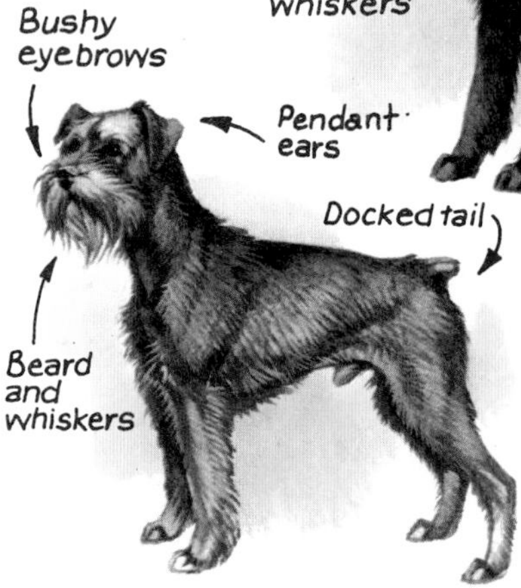

Bushy eyebrows

Pendant ears

Docked tail

Beard and whiskers

◀ Standard Schnauzer

Originally from Germany. Once used to kill pests, e.g. rats. Lively Terrier and good watch dog. Wiry coat. Black or "salt-and-pepper." 18-20 inches high.

Docked tail

Miniature Schnauzer ▶

Also from Germany. Small version of Schnauzer. Rough, hard coat. Black or "salt-and-pepper" color. 12-14 inches high.

Guard dogs

Spectacle markings around eyes

Keeshond ▶

Originally from Holland, where it was used to guard barges. Sometimes called "Dutch Barge Dog." Has a fox-like head and a neck ruff. Long coat. Gray, with cream legs and feet.
16-19 inches high.

Feathering on thighs

Docked tail

◀ Schipperke

Originally from Belgium, also called "Belgian Barge Dog." Short, smooth coat, longer on the neck. Usually black.
12-13 inches high.

Massive head

Bulldog ▶

A famous British breed. Brave and determined. Once used for bull-baiting. Big head for its body. Friendly. Short coat. Any color but black. Weight up to 55 pounds.

Front legs wide apart

Gun dogs

These dogs have been bred to help the hunter. Some are used to find and flush (frighten out) game. Others are taught to "stay" until an animal is shot; they then go to fetch it (called retrieving) for the hunter.

Drentse Patrijshond ▶
Originally from Holland. Good at hunting partridge. Can retrieve game from water. Thick, longish coat. White with brown or orange marks. 22-25 inches high.

Ears feathered →

Long, feathered tail

◀ Britanny Spaniel
Originally from Britanny. Fast, intelligent gun dog. Fairly smooth coat. White with orange or brown colors. 18-20 inches high.

Ears hang flat →

Large Münsterlander ▶
Originally from Germany. Good gundog and pest-catcher. Long, smooth, slightly wavy coat. White with black patches. 23-25 inches high.

Gun dogs

Welsh Springer Spaniel ▶

Originally from Wales. Smaller than the English Springer. Will retrieve shot birds from water. Has a straight, thick, silky coat. Red and white coloring. 18-19 inches high.

Docked tail

◀ English Springer Spaniel

One of the older breeds of spaniel. Can find, drive out, and retrieve game. Active dog. Usually liver and white or black and white. 20 inches high.

Top-knot of curly hair

Short, smooth tip to tail

Irish Water Spaniel ▶

A very old breed. Hard worker. Good at retrieving game from water. Brave. Stiff, short curly coat. Dark liver color. 20-23 inches high.

Gun dogs

Cocker Spaniel ▶

Originally from Britain. Most popular breed of spaniel. Kept for showing and as a house dog. Longish coat. Many colors such as black, red, golden or liver. 15-19 inches high.

Long, drooping, pendant ears

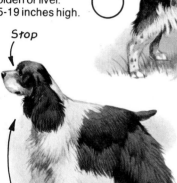

Stop

◀ American Cocker Spaniel

Very different from the English Cocker: smaller, with round head and thick coat. Coat feathered on body and legs. Mixed colors, black or buff. 13-15 inches high.

Long, drooping, pendant ears

Field Spaniel ▶

Originally from Britain. Lower and longer than other Spaniels. Coat medium long. All colors, but often black, red, liver or roan. 18 inches high.

Long body

Shorter legs than other spaniels

Gun dogs

Sussex Spaniel ▶

Originally from England. Rare. Easy to train. Heavy, with shorter legs than other Spaniels. Always liver, gold tips. 15-16 inches high.

Docked tail

Always this color

Docked tail

Long, heavy body

◀ Clumber Spaniel

Originally from Clumber Park, England. Heavy, with short legs. Close, silky coat. White with lemon markings. 44-71 lbs. weight.

Short legs

Long tail

Small Münsterlander ▶

Originally from Westphalia, Germany. Can find and retrieve game. Long, wavy coat. White and brown, roan marks. 19-22 inches high.

Deep chest

Gun dogs

Chesapeake Bay Retriever ▶

Originally from the East
coast (USA). Intelligent.
Short, wavy coat.
Dark brown
to faded tan.
21-26 inches high.

*Short coat,
slightly wavy*

◀ Labrador Retriever

Probably from Newfound-
land. Popular gun dog and
house dog; also used by
police. Short, thick coat.
Black, yellow or
chocolate.
21-22 inches high.

Curly coat

Curly-coated Retriever ▶

British working dog. Big,
strong gun dog. Can retrieve
from water. Coat of tight
curls. Black or
liver color.
25-27 inches high.

Gun dogs

Flat-coated Retriever ▶

A British breed. Good retrieving dog. Strong and intelligent. Flat, springy coat. Black or liver color. 20-24 inches high.

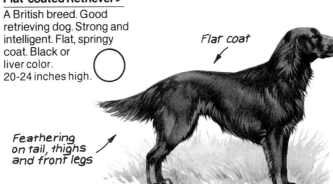

Flat coat

Feathering on tail, thighs and front legs

Flat or wavy coat with feathering

◀ Golden Retriever

A very popular breed. Works well. A good house dog. Flat or wavy coat. Any shade of of cream or gold. 20-24 inches high.

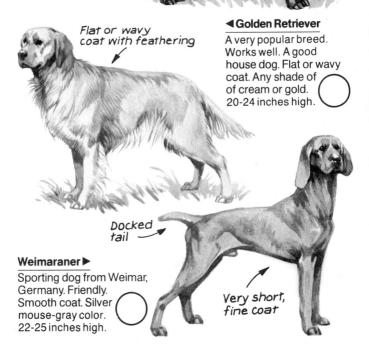

Docked tail

Weimaraner ▶

Sporting dog from Weimar, Germany. Friendly. Smooth coat. Silver mouse-gray color. 22-25 inches high.

Very short, fine coat

Gun dogs

English Setter ▶
Old British gun dog breed.
Long, silky coat; slightly
wavy. Black and white,
lemon and white, liver
and white,
tricolor.
24-27 inches high.

Stop

Long, silky
wavy coat

Feathering
on legs and tail

Feathering
on legs and tail

◀ Gordon Setter
Originally from Scotland.
Heavy breed. Rather self-
willed. Long, soft and
glossy coat. Shiny black
with tan
markings.
26 inches high.

Stop

Always this
color

Irish Setter ▶
Originally from Ireland.
Works well when trained.
Has a long neck and head.
Long, silky coat.
Always chestnut.
24 inches high.

Deep
chest

Gun dogs

Vizsla ▶
Originally from Hungary. Finds and retrieves shot game birds. Short coated. Sandy yellow. 22-25 inches high.

Long, drooping, pendant ears

Always this color

Short, glossy coat

◀ Pointer
Originally from Spain. Will "point" at a game bird with nose, body and tail in a straight line. Short, smooth coat. Black, or another color with white. 24-27 inches high.

Long, tapering tail

Docked tail

German
Short-haired Pointer ▶
Originally from Germany. Finds and retrieves game. Friendly. Short, hard coat. Liver, or liver-and-white spotted or ticked. 25-26 inches high.

Companion dogs

Many of these breeds were originally working breeds but they are now all kept as house pets. They make good companion dogs.

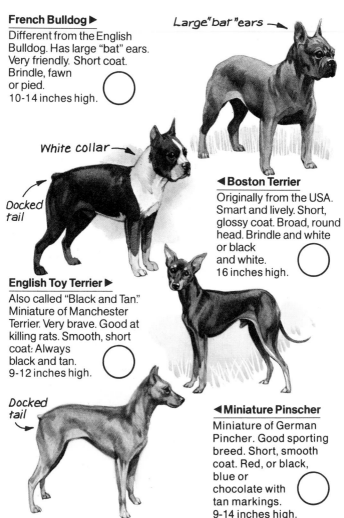

French Bulldog ▶

Different from the English Bulldog. Has large "bat" ears. Very friendly. Short coat. Brindle, fawn or pied.
10-14 inches high.

Large "bat" ears →

White collar →

Docked tail

◀ Boston Terrier

Originally from the USA. Smart and lively. Short, glossy coat. Broad, round head. Brindle and white or black and white.
16 inches high.

English Toy Terrier ▶

Also called "Black and Tan." Miniature of Manchester Terrier. Very brave. Good at killing rats. Smooth, short coat. Always black and tan.
9-12 inches high.

Docked tail

◀ Miniature Pinscher

Miniature of German Pincher. Good sporting breed. Short, smooth coat. Red, or black, blue or chocolate with tan markings.
9-14 inches high.

Companion dogs

Pug ▶
Originally from China. King William III brought them to the English Court in the 17th century. Friendly pet. Short, glossy coat. Fawn or black. 13 inches high.

Tail curls over hip

Wrinkles

Black mouth

◀ Chow Chow
Originally a temple dog from China; now a popular pet. Looks like a lion. Long thick coat. Black, red, blue, fawn or cream in color. 18 inches high.

Tufted tail

Löwchen ▶
"Little Lion Dog." Old and rare breed. Probably comes from the Mediterranean. Long coat. Good temperament. Usually black, white, gray or cream. 10 inches high.

Crest of hair

Hair

A little hair on feet

◀ Chinese Crested Dog
This breed may originally have come from Mexico or Africa. Almost hairless. Pink, blue, mauve or white, patches. 13 inches high.

Companion dogs

Cavalier King Charles Spaniel ▶

Originally from Britain. Long, silky coat. Black and tan, red and white, red or tricolor. Weighs up to 17½ lbs.

Long, feathered ears

Short Muzzle

◀ King Charles Spaniel

Favorite at the court of King Charles II. Smaller than the cavalier. Long, silky coat. Black and tan, rich red or tricolor. Weighs up to 13 lbs.

Tibetan Spaniel ▶

Originally bred by monks in Tibet. Looks like the Pekingese. Long, smooth coat. Golden, cream, white, black or tricolor. 9-11 inches high.

Curled tail

◀ Bichon Frisé

Probably from Spain. Toy dog. Silky white coat; often has gray patches on the skin. 8-12 inches high.

Silky, white hair

Companion dogs

Rounded skull

Japanese Chin ▶
Toy dog, probably from China. Once a favorite of Japanese emperors. Long coat. White with red, black patches. 12 inches high.

◄ Large, feathered ears

◄ Papillon
Called "Butterfly Dog" because of the shape of its head and ears. Originally from France. Long coat. White with all colors except liver. Up to 11 inches high.

Pomeranian ▶
A miniature Spitz from Pomerania. Popular toy dog. Long coat. Red, blue, orange, white, black or brown. Up to 11 inches high.

◄ Tail lies flat over the back

Mane

◄ Affenpinscher
Tiny dog from Germany. Often shown in old Dutch paintings. Looks like a monkey. Wiry coat and usually black. Up to 11 inches high.

Companion dogs

Beard and whiskers

Tail curls over back

Shih Tzu ▶
Originally from China.
Tiny but brave. Rounded
skull, square muzzle. Long
straight coat.
All colors.
Up to 11 inches high.

Feathered tail arched over back

◀ Maltese
Very old toy breed from
Malta. Often painted in
pictures as a lap dog.
Short body and legs.
Long, pure-
white coat.
7-10 inches high.

Pekingese ▶
Originally from China,
where it was once a court
pet. Long Coat. All colors
except
liver.
6-10 inches high.

Tail curled over back

Beard and whiskers

◀ Lhasa Apso
Originally from Tibet. Lively
breed. Often seen at
shows. Long, hard coat.
Usually golden,
sandy or gray.
9-11 inches high.

Companion dogs

Australian Silky Terrier ▶
Bred in Australia from
Yorkshire and Australian
Terriers. Long, silky coat.
Silver, or blue
with tan marks.
8 inches high.

Small, erect ears

Yorkshire Terrier ▶ ◀

Very long coat with parting in the middle

◀ Yorkshire Terrier
Tiny English Terrier. Very
popular toy dog. Good
pest-catcher. Long,
straight, silky coat. Should
be dark blue and
tan colored.
7-8 inches high.

Griffon Bruxellois ▶
Also called "Brussels
Griffon." Originally from
Belgium. Lively toy dog.
Rough, wiry, short coat.
Red, black or black
and tan.
Up to 10 lbs.
weight.

Docked tail

Semi-erect ears

Heavy whiskers

Short, smooth coat

Docked tail

◀ Griffon Brabançon
Also called "Smooth
Griffon." Comes from
Belgium. Like Griffon
Bruxellois, but smooth-
coated. Colors like
Bruxellois.
Up to
10 lbs. weight.

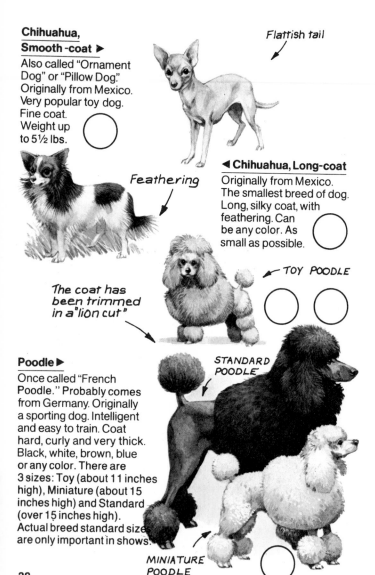

Chihuahua, Smooth-coat ▶

Also called "Ornament Dog" or "Pillow Dog." Originally from Mexico. Very popular toy dog. Fine coat. Weight up to 5½ lbs.

Flattish tail

Feathering

◀ Chihuahua, Long-coat

Originally from Mexico. The smallest breed of dog. Long, silky coat, with feathering. Can be any color. As small as possible.

The coat has been trimmed in a "lion cut"

TOY POODLE

Poodle ▶

Once called "French Poodle." Probably comes from Germany. Originally a sporting dog. Intelligent and easy to train. Coat hard, curly and very thick. Black, white, brown, blue or any color. There are 3 sizes: Toy (about 11 inches high), Miniature (about 15 inches high) and Standard (over 15 inches high). Actual breed standard size are only important in shows.

STANDARD POODLE

MINIATURE POODLE

Hunting terriers

Terriers are small and active dogs. They were used to chase animals, such as foxes and badgers, down holes. Nearly all breeds of terrier originally came from the British Isles.

West Highland
White Terrier ▶

Originally from Scotland. Popular house pet. Good guard. Long, coarse coat, soft undercoat. Always white.
Up to 11 inches high.

Small, upright tail

◀ Scottish Terrier

Once called "Aberdeen Terrier." Show dog and pet. Intelligent. Wiry, longish coat. Black, flecked gray or brown.
9-11 inches high.

Sealyham Terrier ▶

Originally from Wales where it was used for hunting in packs. Difficult to train. Long, wiry coat. White, sometimes with yellow markings on head and ears.
Up to 12 inches high.

Slightly curved head

Small, pointed, erect ears ➔

◀ Cairn Terrier

Originally from Scotland. Very similar to the West Highland White. One of the smallest terriers. Longish, hard coat. Red, sandy, gray, mottled brown or off-black.
9-10 inches high.

Hunting terriers

Norwich Terrier & Norfolk Terrier ▶

Very similar breeds. Both come from East Anglia, England. Norwich has upright ears; Norfolk has semi-erect ears. Wiry coat. Red, black and tan, sandy or grayish color. 10 inches high.

Docked tail

Erect ears

◀ Border Terrier

Often used by hunters in Britain. Very active breed. Rough, weatherproof coat. Red, wheaten, gray and tan or blue and tan color. 10-12 inches high.

Erect ears

Docked tail

Australian Terrier ▶

Popular in Australia and New Zealand. Strong and friendly. Hard, straight coat. Red, or blue and tan in color. 10 inches high.

Large, wide head

Curved tail

◀ Dandie Dinmont Terrier

Named after a character in a novel by Sir Walter Scott. Coat of mixed soft and hard hairs. Pepper or mustard color. 8-11 inches high.

Hunting terriers

Airedale Terrier ▶
Named after Aire Valley, Yorkshire. Largest Terrier. Used to hunt pests. Strong, but easy to train. Rough, wiry coat. Black or gray and tan. 21-24 inches high.

Semi-erect ears →

Long head

◀ Lakeland Terrier
Used for hunting in North of England. Smaller than Airedale. Rough, thick coat. Various colors. 14 inches high.

Semi-erect ears carried forward

Beard and whiskers

Beard and whiskers

Welsh Terrier ▶
Used in Wales to hunt. Strong. Good as guard dog and house dog. Hard, wiry coat. Black and tan. 15 inches high.

Blue color

◀ Kerry Blue Terrier
Originally from Ireland where it hunted fox, badger and otter. Popular show dog. Bright and friendly. Soft wavy coat. Any blue shade. 17-19 inches high.

Hunting terriers

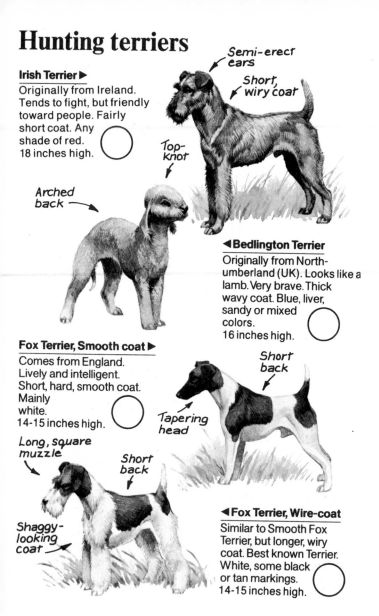

Irish Terrier ▶
Originally from Ireland.
Tends to fight, but friendly
toward people. Fairly
short coat. Any
shade of red.
18 inches high.

Semi-erect ears

Short, wiry coat

Top-knot

Arched back

◀ Bedlington Terrier
Originally from North-
umberland (UK). Looks like a
lamb. Very brave. Thick
wavy coat. Blue, liver,
sandy or mixed
colors.
16 inches high.

Fox Terrier, Smooth coat ▶
Comes from England.
Lively and intelligent.
Short, hard, smooth coat.
Mainly
white.
14-15 inches high.

Short back

Tapering head

Long, square muzzle

Short back

Shaggy-looking coat

◀ Fox Terrier, Wire-coat
Similar to Smooth Fox
Terrier, but longer, wiry
coat. Best known Terrier.
White, some black
or tan markings.
14-15 inches high.

Hunting terriers

Manchester Terrier ▶

Originally from the North of
England where it was used
to catch rats. Intelligent
and lively. Short, glossy
coat. Black with
tan markings.
15-16 inches high.

Short, glossy coat

Egg-shaped head

◀ Bull Terrier

Originally from the English
Midlands. Tends to fight
other dogs. Friendly with
people. Short, smooth
coat. White, sometimes
with markings,
or colored.
16 inches high.

Semi-erect ears

Staffordshire Bull Terrier ▶

Fighting dog from the English
Midlands. Friendly with
children. Short, glossy
coat. Red, fawn,
blue or black.
14-16 inches high.

Short legs

◀ Jack Russell Terrier

Not recognized by any
kennel club. Name often
used incorrectly for several
types of small Terrier.
Usually short coated.
White with
colored
patches.

Hauling dogs

These dogs were once used to pull sleds over snow and ice in the Arctic. They were specially bred for this job. Today, snowmobiles are often used instead of sleds.

Alaskan Malamute ▶

Named after an Eskimo tribe. Large, strong dog. Intelligent. Thick coat. Gray to black, white under body. 20-25 inches high.

Mask-like markings on head

Tail curves over the back

◀ Siberian Husky

Once used in Siberia for herding, sled hauling and as house dog. Good working dog. Long, thick but soft coat. All colors, with white markings. 20-23 inches high.

Small, erect ears ⟶

Tail curves over back ⟶

Samoyed ▶

Originally from Russia. Still used in sled races. Can round up reindeer. Long, straight coat. Silvery white; may have cream marks. 18-21 inches high.

Scent hunters

These dogs have a good sense of smell. They use their noses to track down prey. In their home countries they are popular for hunting.

Elkhound ▶

Originally from Norway, where it was used to hunt Elk. Can stand cold weather. Thick, hard coat. Gray color. 18-20 inches high.

Erect, pointed ears

Tightly curled tail

Ridge of hair on back ends in two "scrolls" on withers

◀ Rhodesian Ridgeback

Originally from Zimbabwe. Used to guard and hunt. Strong fighter. Short, glossy coat. Yellowish to reddish color. 24-27 inches high.

Tail curled onto thigh

Finnish Spitz ▶

Originally from Finland, where it was used for hunting. Good guard. Noisy. Longish coat. Red-gold to red-brown. 15-17 inches high.

Mane

Scent hunters

Basset Hound ▶
Originally from France.
Good natured. Smooth,
short coat. Can be
any recognized
hound color.
13-15 inches high.

Very long,
pendant
ears

Long, pendant
ears

Short legs

◀ Basset Griffon Vendéen
Originally from southwest
France, where it was used
for hunting hares.
Longish coat. Mostly white,
with colored
markings.
13-17 inches high.

Tail carried high

Beagle ▶
Originally from England;
Queen Elizabeth I hunted
with Beagles. Popular,
friendly house dog. Short,
hard coat. Any
hound color.
13-16 inches high.

Tail
tightly
curled

◀ Basenji
Originally from Congo area,
Africa, where it was used
to hunt antelope. Black,
red, chestnut and white,
or black and tan
with white.
16-17 inches high.

Scent hunters

Bloodhound ▶
Brought to England in William the Conqueror's time. Hunted deer. Good sense of smell and used by police to track criminals. Short, glossy coat. Black or liver and tan, sometimes red. 24-26 inches high.

Very long, pendant ears →

↑ Loose skin on the head

Long tail →

◀ Foxhound
Often used in packs for hunting. Friendly. Short, smooth coat. Usually tan with black and white markings, or white with black, tan or lemon marks. 21-25 inches high.

Rough coat

Otterhound ▶
A British breed bred to hunt otters. Swims well. Longish, hard coat. Usually fawn or grey with black and tan markings. 24-26 inches high.

Scent hunters

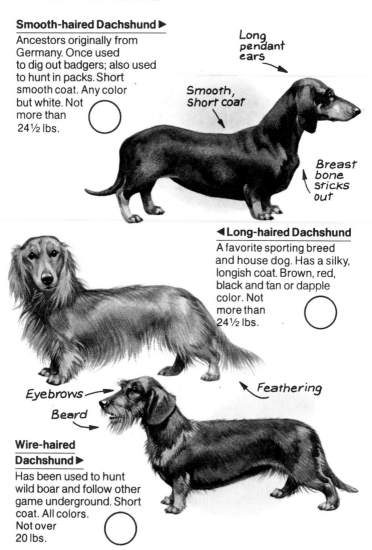

Smooth-haired Dachshund ▶

Ancestors originally from
Germany. Once used
to dig out badgers; also used
to hunt in packs. Short
smooth coat. Any color
but white. Not
more than
24½ lbs.

Long
pendant
ears

Smooth,
Short coat

Breast
bone
Sticks
out

◀ Long-haired Dachshund

A favorite sporting breed
and house dog. Has a silky,
longish coat. Brown, red,
black and tan or dapple
color. Not
more than
24½ lbs.

Eyebrows

Beard

Feathering

Wire-haired Dachshund ▶

Has been used to hunt
wild boar and follow other
game underground. Short
coat. All colors.
Not over
20 lbs.

Pedigrees, crossbreds, mongrels

A pedigree is a "family tree" which records a dog's breeding history. If a dog has ancestors of the same breed that have been recorded for at least three generations, it is a **pedigree dog**.

Dogs' pedigrees have been kept for centuries, especially in the Far East and the Middle East. Today registers of pedigrees are kept by kennel clubs and special societies such as the American or Canadian Kennel Club. Dog owners usually register pedigree puppies soon after they are born. If you buy a pedigree puppy, you will be given its pedigree history written down on a special certificate.

A dog with parents of the same breed is **purebred.** If a dog's parents are of different breeds it is a **crossbred.** This is not the same as a mongrel. A **mongrel** is a dog of mixed breed whose parents are either not known, or are crossbred.

The family tree of a crossbred dog

Purebred parent

Purebred parent

Crossbred dog

The family tree of a pedigree dog

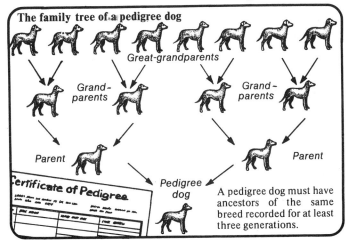

Great-grandparents

Grand-parents

Grand-parents

Parent

Parent

Certificate of Pedigree

Pedigree dog

A pedigree dog must have ancestors of the same breed recorded for at least three generations.

Choosing a puppy

Think carefully before you choose a puppy. Do not buy the first cuddly puppy you see.

Choose a healthy puppy

Does it have all its teeth?

Is its coat healthy?

Are the eyes bright?

Are the ears clean inside?

Before you buy a dog ask yourself some of these questions: Where will you keep it – in a small apartment or a large yard? How often will you be able to exercise it? Can you afford to feed it? Do you want a dog or a bitch? Will you mind finding dog hair in the house? Do you want the dog as a pet, or a guard dog, or both? Are you looking for a pedigree dog or a mongrel?

Now work out which breeds fit your needs. Look at the dogs in this book. Go to a big dog show. When you have chosen a breed, buy your puppy from a breeding kennel which specializes in that breed.

First choice: lively and friendly

Possibly too shy

Choosing the right puppy

Choose a lively puppy that shows interest in you, but try not to choose a very bold pup (it may be difficult to train) or a very shy pup (it may stay nervous all its life). Do not buy if any of the puppies look ill.

50

Feeding your dog

A well-fed dog looks fit and healthy. Its diet must include protein, minerals, vitamins and energy foods. Some processed dog foods contain all these items in the right amounts, but if you feed your dog cooked meat, you must add dry dog food (kibble) and minerals and vitamins. Never give your dog raw meat as it carries the parasite toxoplasmosis. Bonemeal will give the dog the calcium it needs. It is dangerous to give bones to your dog as they are likely to splinter and cause internal injuries.

Take care not to overfeed your dog by giving it leftovers and feeding it between meals.

If you are worried about your dog's food, ask a vet. Puppies have special feeding needs; contact your vet if you want more advice.

The amount of food you give your dog depends on the type of food, the size of the dog, and the amount of exercise it gets. Below are some examples. There are 3 common types of dog food: dry, semimoist, and canned. Dry food is necessary for clean teeth; oil and animal fat (lard) keep a dog's coat glossy. Dog biscuits may be substituted for dry food, as a treat.

This is the approximate amount of food you should give your dog each day; the less exercise your dog gets, the less food it needs.

MINIATURE DACHSHUND

4 oz
dry
food

or

6 oz
meat and
biscuit

or

12 oz
canned
food

FOX TERRIER

8 oz
dry
food

or

11 oz
meat and
biscuit

or

1 lb 3.5 oz
canned
food

LABRADOR

1 lb
dry
food

or

1 lb 3.5 oz
meat and
biscuit

or

3 lb 5 oz
canned
food

GREAT DANE

1 lb 9 oz
dry
food

or

2 lb 10.5 oz
meat and
biscuit

or

5 lb 8.5 oz
canned
food

Grooming your dog

Get your puppy used to being groomed as soon as possible. If your dog has a short coat, use a grooming-glove. Short coated dogs need brushing once or twice a week. If your dog has a long coat you will need a short-bristled brush and a steel comb. Long haired dogs need brushing daily. Use the comb first, then the brush. Catch any loose hairs in a newspaper and discard them. Dogs such as poodles and some terriers will need to have their coats clipped regularly.

Dogs over six months old should be bathed as needed. Use a special dog shampoo. Do not use a detergent, carbolic or disinfectant. Dry the dog with its own towel to stop it from getting a chill

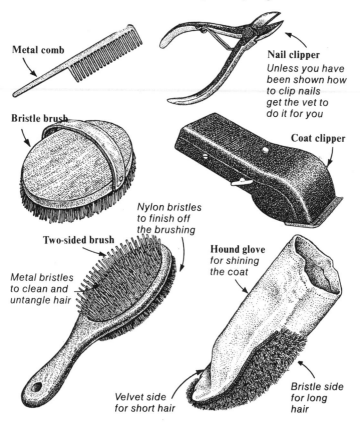

Metal comb

Nail clipper
Unless you have been shown how to clip nails get the vet to do it for you

Bristle brush

Coat clipper

Nylon bristles to finish off the brushing

Two-sided brush

Metal bristles to clean and untangle hair

Hound glove
for shining the coat

Velvet side for short hair

Bristle side for long hair

Showing your dog

Showing a dog can be great fun. At dog shows you will meet other dog lovers and will have all the excitement of preparing your dog, parading it in the show ring, and perhaps winning a prize.

You can find out about local dog shows from advertisements in the dog magazines. It is a good idea to visit some shows before you enter your own dog. There you will find out what the judges are looking for, and will pick up tips about training, preparing and showing your breed of dog. For showing, your dog must be well groomed, healthy and obedient.

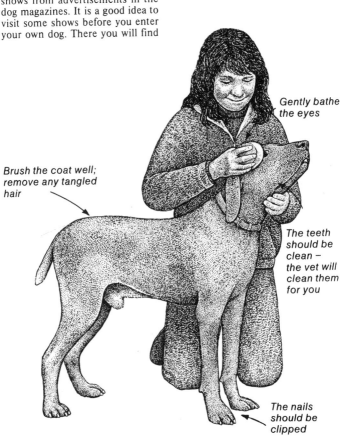

Gently bathe the eyes

Brush the coat well; remove any tangled hair

The teeth should be clean – the vet will clean them for you

The nails should be clipped

Illness

When you get a dog, take it to a vet as soon as possible. The vet will give the dog its shots and check its health.

Always contact the vet if your dog shows signs of being sick. A dog may be sick if it behaves strangely, is very sluggish and inactive and spends a lot of time asleep, has bad diarrhea, scratches a lot, keeps shaking its head or rubbing its face on the ground, or smells unpleasant.

It will certainly need urgent treatment if it has a high temperature, bloody diarrhea, fits, or if it cannot pass urine.

Your puppy should be vaccinated against distemper, hepatitis, para-influenza, parvovirus, and rabies. Your dog should be checked for heartworm every spring and medicated accordingly; and once a year a stool sample should be examined for worms.

Do remember: **if your dog is sick, contact the vet.**

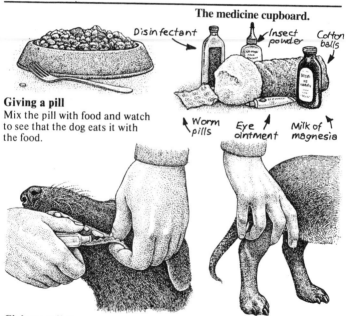

The medicine cupboard.

Disinfectant · Insect powder · Cotton balls · Worm pills · Eye ointment · Milk of magnesia

Giving a pill
Mix the pill with food and watch to see that the dog eats it with the food.

Giving medicine
Using a small bottle, pour medicine into a pouch made by holding the dog's lips.

Taking a pulse
Take the pulse inside the thigh. It should be about 70-90 beats per minute.

Understanding your dog

The ancestors of domestic dogs lived in packs with a leader dog. Your dog will see you as its leader and will expect to obey you. Training is therefore very important and if it is done correctly the dog will enjoy the sessions.

A dog cannot understand what you are saying to it but it can interpret and remember sounds and tones of voice. It can remember the sounds of commands such as "sit", "down", etc. and the sound of its name, but it cannot understand language.

If your dog is naughty never hit it or shout at it. The first time you need to scold your dog shake it by the scruff of the neck and say "no!" in a stern voice. The dog will then associate the word no with scolding.

Body language

A dog shows how it feels by the position of its body. Here are some common body postures.

Playful
This dog is asking for a game

Alert position

Aggressive
The body becomes stiff and the hair bristles

On guard

Afraid

The tail falls between the legs

Training your dog

Training your dog will take a long time and you will need a lot of patience. You must never get angry or lose your temper. First get the puppy used to the sound of your voice. It will soon be able to tell by the tone of your voice when you are pleased with it and when you are scolding it. Teach the puppy its name as soon as you can. Choose a short, simple name.

Start training sessions when the puppy is young, but keep them very short. Commands should be simple. Stick to words such as "no", "sit", "stay", "come", and use a different tone of voice for each command. Affection is the best reward.

Your puppy will have to be house-trained. The safest way is to put it outside immediately after each meal. If possible, take it to a special spot in the yard; otherwise teach it to use the gutter in a quiet street. Always clean up after your dog; in many places it's the law.

You can stop your dog from jumping up by raising your knee

To teach your dog to sit, press it on its back and say "sit"

Press the dog's back

A dog owner's code

1 **DO** license your dog.
2 **DO** feed your dog at regular times. Do not give it tidbits between meals.
3 **DO** feed your dog from its own bowl. Wash it and keep it apart from the family dishes.
4 **DO** keep your dog clean.
5 **DO NOT** let your dog be noisy and disturb your neighbors.

Make sure your dog has a strong collar.

Tag with owner's name and address, dog license, rabies tag.

6 **DO** make proper arrangements for looking after your dog when you go away on vacation.
7 **DO** be sure that your dogs has its shots and rabies tag.

Never let your dog hang its head out of the car window.

8 **DO** keep your dog on a leash when it is near streets or in towns.
9 **DO NOT** take your dog into food stores or restaurants.

Keep your dog on its leash in the street.

10 **DO NOT** let your dog roam free.
11 **DO NOT** let your dog bother people. Some people dislike dogs, and children may be frightened by them.
12 **DO** train your dog to obey you.
13 **DO always** clean up after your dog.
14 **DO** see the vet if you do not want your dog to have puppies.
15 **DO NOT ever** leave your dog in a car with the windows shut.

Working dogs

The Border Collie is gazing steadily at the group of sheep to hold them still

The owner is giving a hand signal to the Labrador

Sheep dogs

Dogs have been used for centuries to look after sheep and cattle. They are trained to fetch, drive and guide the animals. Sheep dogs include the Border Collie, the German Shepherd, and the Kelpie.

Gun dogs

Retrievers and spaniels sit until the game has been shot; they retrieve the dead animal and drop it in front of the hunter at a hand signal. They are also used to flush (frighten out) game. Setters and pointers "point" out the position of game with their heads.

This dog has been taught to attack the arm of a moving criminal

This guide dog has taken its owner to a pedestrian crossing

Police dogs

Police forces all over the world use dogs to help them. Their favorite breed is the German Shepherd. They also use Labradors, Dobermanns, Rottweilers and other large breeds that are strong and intelligent. They are taught to attack a moving criminal.

Guide dog

The dog wears a special harness around the shoulders. This has a handle that the blind person holds when the dog is guiding its owner. As puppies, guide dogs (seeing eye dogs) live in a town so they get used to town noises. They then have about five months of special training.

Glossary

Beard - thick hair on the muzzle and chin.
Bat ears - broad, upright ears with round tips.
Bitch - female dog.
Blaze - white marking up the face and between the eyes.
Boar - wild pig.
Coursing - chasing game animals (usually hares) for sport.
Cropped ears - ears from which the hanging part has been cut off.
Distemper - dog disease: cough, catarrh and weakness.
Docked tail - dog's tail from which part has been cut off, usually for fashion.
Elk - a very large deer.
Feathering - long, fine fringe of hair.
Game - animals hunted for sport or food; e.g., pheasants, partridges.
Heartworm – parasite carried by mosquitoes; fatal if untreated.
Hepatitis - illness of the liver.

Mask – dark color on the muzzle.
Muzzle - the snout of the animal, including the nose and mouth.
Parvovirus – a virus causing severe, bloody diarrhea; often fatal.
Pests - animals thought of by humans as destructive or harmful.
Ruff - thick hair around the neck.
Spectacles – rings around the eyes.
Spitz - small dog with erect ears, harsh coat and curled tail.
Toy dog – very small breed.
Undercoat – soft, furry hair under the outer hair of some breeds.
Vitamins - nutrients present in tiny amounts in some food; they are vital for normal growth.
Vulva - the sexual opening to the passage which leads to the womb of a female dog.

Colors

Black and tan - a black dog with tan markings, usually on the head, legs and chest.
Blue – bluish-gray.
Brindle - a mixture of light and dark hair, usually dark stripes on a light ground.
Gold – amber or honey color.
Grizzle – iron-gray.
Harlequin - patchy coat, usually black, gray and white.
Lemon - pale yellowish-fawn.
Liver - dark reddish-brown.
Mauve – pinkish-gray.
Merle - bluish-gray streaked with black.

Mustard - yellowish-fawn.
Orange - dark reddish-gold.
Pepper - pale, warm gray.
Pied - two colors in uneven patches.
Pink – pinkish-gray.
Roan – a mixture of white and colored hair.
Sable – black hair on a light, reddish color.
Silver - pale gray.
Tan - pale, warm brown.
Ticked - covered with small spots.
Tricolor - mixture of black, tan and white hairs.
Wheaten - pale fawn.

Books to read

Understanding Dogs. Su Swallow (Hayes Books). All about dog behavior and caring for your dog; also about working dogs.

The American Dog Book. Kurt Unkelbach (Dutton). A history and description of all the recognized breeds in the USA and Canada. There is a general discussion and a photo of each breed. Also advice on choosing a puppy, feeding and training, and facts about dog shows.

Complete Book of Dog Care. Leon F. Whitney, DVM (Doubleday). A home guide to dog care; discusses dog anatomy, diseases of dogs and how to recognize them, how to choose a vet, and general care and feeding of your dog. A helpful, all-purpose book.

The Dog In Your Life. Matthew Margolis and Catherine Swan (Random House). A guide to choosing, raising, feeding and training; includes a special section on traveling with your dog (spells out various state regulations concerning dogs). Helpful photos.

Good Dog, Bad Dog. Mordecai Siegal and Matthew Margolis (Signet). A basic obedience course – easy to use; paperback with photos.

In addition, TFH Books publishes a *This is the...* series for many breeds. These are comprehensive books and go into great detail about the individual breed. All have photos, some in color.

Dog World. 10060 West Roosevelt Road, Westchester, Illinois 60153; a monthly magazine.

Clubs to join

Joining a club is worthwhile because you will be able to find out more about your particular breed of dog. You will also meet other dog owners and be able to enter competitions. There is a dog club or association for nearly every breed of dog – from Airedales to Yorkshire Terriers. You can get the addresses from the American or Canadian Kennel Club. Many associations sponsor shows or have meetings and other interesting activities.

American Kennel Club, 51 Madison Avenue, New York, NY 10010; (212) 696-8292. Founded in 1884; an association of 372 all-breed, specialty breed, and obedience dog clubs. The AKC maintains stud book registry with pedigree records of over 13 million dogs; they also have a library of over 15 thousand books and a breeder information service.

Canadian Kennel Club, 2150 Bloor Street, W., Toronto, Ontario M6S 4V7. Founded in 1888. An association of individuals and clubs that is similar to the American Kennel Club, in that they are a registry and regulatory agency for the sport of dogs in Canada.

Westminster Kennel Club, 230 Park Ave., Ste. 644 New York, NY 10169 (212) 682-6852. Founded in 1877. Sponsors annual dog show (very famous and popular) for owners and exhibitors of more than 100 breeds.

Scorecard

The dogs in this scorecard are arranged in alphabetical order. When you spot a particular breed, fill in the date next to its name. You can add up your score after a day out spotting.

	Score	Date seen		Score	Date seen
Affenpinscher	25		Chow Chow	10	
Alaskan Malamute	5		Collie, Bearded	10	
Anatolian Karabash	25		Collie, Border	10	
Basenji	10		Collie, Rough	5	
Basset Griffon Vendéen	25		Collie, Smooth	10	
Beagle	5		Corgi, Cardigan	10	
Belgian Malinois	20		Corgi, Pembroke	5	
Belgian Sheepdog	20		Dachsund, Long-haired	10	
Belgian Tervuren	25		Dachsund, Smooth-haired	5	
Bichon Frisé	15		Dachsund, Wire-haired	15	
Bloodhound	15		Dalmation	5	
Borzoi	10		Deerhound	20	
Bouvier des Flandres	20		Dobermann	5	
Boxer	5		Drentse Patrijshond	25	
Briard	15		Elkhound	10	
Bulldog	10		Foxhound	15	
Bulldog, French	20		German Shepherd Dog	5	
Bullmastiff	10		Great Dane	5	
Cattle Dog, Australian	25		Great Pyrenees	20	
Chihuahua, Long-coat	5		Griffon Brabançon	20	
Chihuahua, Smooth-coat	5		Griffon Bruxellois	20	
Chinese Crested Dog	25		Greyhound	10	

	Score	Date seen		Score	Date seen
Greyhound, Italian	15		Pekingese	5	
Hound, Afghan	5		Pinscher, Miniature	15	
Hound, Basset	5		Pointer	10	
Hound, Ibizan	20		Pointer, German Short-haired	5	
Hound, Pharaoh	25		Pomeranian	10	
Husky, Siberian	5		Poodle, Miniature	5	
Japanese Chin	20		Poodle, Standard	10	
Keeshound	10		Poodle, Toy	5	
Kelpie	25		Pug	10	
Komondor	20		Puli	20	
Kuvasz	20		Retriever, Chesapeake Bay	15	
Leonberger	25		Retriever, Curly-coated	20	
Lhasa Apso	5		Retriever, Flat-coated	20	
Löwchen	20		Retriever, Golden	5	
Lurcher	25		Retriever, Labrador	5	
Maltese	15		Rhodesian Ridgeback	10	
Maremma	25		Rottweiler	10	
Mountain Dog, Bernese	20		St. Bernard	5	
Mountain Dog, Estrela	25		Saluki	15	
Munsterlander, Large	25		Samoyed	10	
Munsterlander, Small	25		Schipperke	15	
Newfoundland	10		Schnauzer, Giant	15	
Norwegian Buhund	25		Schnauzer, Miniature	10	
Otterhound	20		Schnauzer, Standard	20	
Papillon	20		Setter, English	10	

	Score	Date seen		Score	Date seen
Setter, Gordon	15		Terrier, Bull	15	
Setter, Irish	5		Terrier, Cairn	10	
Sheepdog, Old English	5		Terrier, Dandie Dinmont	20	
Sheepdog, Shetland	5		Terrier, English Toy	20	
Shih Tzu	5		Terrier, Irish	15	
Sloughi	25		Terrier, Jack Russell	20	
Spaniel, American Cocker	10		Terrier, Kerry Blue	10	
Spaniel, Brittany	15		Terrier, Lakeland	15	
Spaniel, Cavalier King Charles	20		Terrier, Manchester	15	
Spaniel, Clumber	20		Terrier, Norfolk	15	
Spaniel, Cocker	5		Terrier, Norwich	15	
Spaniel, English Springer	10		Terrier, Scottish	10	
Spaniel, Field	20		Terrier, Sealyham	15	
Spaniel, Irish Water	20		Terrier, Smooth Fox	10	
Spaniel, King Charles	20		Terrier, Staffordshire Bull	20	
Spaniel, Sussex	20		Terrier, Tibetan	20	
Spaniel, Tibetan	20		Terrier, Welsh	15	
Spaniel, Welsh Springer	20		Terrier, West Highland White	5	
Spitz, Finnish	25		Terrier, Wire Fox	5	
Terrier, Airedale	10		Terrier, Yorkshire	5	
Terrier, Australian	20		Vallhund	25	
Terrier, Australian Silky	15		Vizsla	15	
Terrier, Bedlington	10		Weimaraner	10	
Terrier, Border	20		Whippet	15	
Terrier, Boston	20		Wolfhound, Irish	15	

Index